Save the Earth!

Ready, Freddy!

Save the Earth!

by ABBY KLEIN

illustrated by JOHN McKINLEY

Scholastic Inc.
New York Toronto London Auckland
Sydney Mexico City New Delhi Hong Kong

To Carol,
the Compost Queen!
Your passion for taking care of our Earth
has inspired me to be more green.
Thanks for being such an amazing teacher!
Love,
A.K.

No part of this publication may be reproduced, stored in a retrieval system, or transmitted in any form or by any means, electronic, mechanical, photocopying, recording, or otherwise, without written permission of the publisher. For information regarding permission, write to Scholastic Inc., Attention: Permissions Department, 557 Broadway, New York, NY 10012.

ISBN 978-0-545-29503-1

12 11 10 9 8   15 16 17/0

Printed in the U.S.A.   40
First printing, January 2012

CHAPTERS

I have a problem.

A really, really big problem.

My teacher, Mrs. Wushy, gave us
an Earth Day Challenge, but I don't
know if I can do all the activities
on the list by Friday.

Let me tell you about it.

CHAPTER 1

What Is Earth Day?

"This Friday is a very special day," said our teacher, Mrs. Wushy.

"I know why! I know why!" said Chloe, waving her painted red fingernails in the air.

"You do?" asked Mrs. Wushy. "Would you like to tell the class why it is so special?"

"Friday is my dance recital, and I am the star of the show!"

"Is she for real?" whispered my best friend, Robbie.

"It's always about her," said Jessie, shaking her head.

"I can do some of my dance for you," said Chloe, jumping up. "Right here. Right now."

"Sit down, Dancypants," said Max. "No one wants to see you dance."

"Says who?" asked Chloe.

"Me!" said Max, getting up out of his seat and walking over to her.

"Get away from me, you big bully," said Chloe.

"Max," said Mrs. Wushy, "please go back and sit down."

"Yeah," said Chloe with her hands on her hips. "Go back and sit down."

"Chloe," said Mrs. Wushy, "you are not the teacher. You both need to sit down."

"But what about my dance?" Chloe whined.

"Maybe you can show us another time," said Mrs. Wushy. "I want to talk about the special day on Friday. I know you have your dance recital on Friday, but that was not what I was thinking of."

"I know why Friday is special," said Robbie. "It's Earth Day."

"Earth Day? What's that?" asked Jessie.

"It's like a holiday, to celebrate our amazing planet, Earth," said Robbie.

"That's right," said Mrs. Wushy. "Earth Day is celebrated each year on April twenty-second."

"Is it kind of like the Earth's birthday?" said Max. "Do you eat cake and ice cream?"

"Oooh. Ice cream," said Chloe. "I love ice cream. Cotton candy is my favorite flavor, because it's pink, and pink is my favorite color."

"You don't eat cake and ice cream on Earth Day," said Mrs. Wushy. "You think about our beautiful planet, and you come up with ways you can help take care of it."

"That sounds cool," said Jessie.

"People all over the world celebrate Earth Day," said Mrs. Wushy.

"When I looked on my computer, I saw that over one hundred countries celebrate it," said Robbie.

"Over one hundred!" I said. "That's a lot."

"What are we going to do to celebrate?" asked Jessie.

"Well, we're going to be doing different activities all week to celebrate and to help the planet," said Mrs. Wushy.

"But what can kids do to help the Earth?" I asked.

"A lot!" said Mrs. Wushy. "Even little things add up to make the world a better place. You'd be surprised."

"Like what?" asked Max.

"You tell me," said Mrs. Wushy.

"I know," said Robbie. "We can recycle."

"I recycle cans at home," said Max.

"You can recycle more than cans," said Mrs. Wushy. "What else can you recycle?"

"We recycle cans, plastic, glass, and paper at my house," said Jessie.

"Us, too!" I said.

"You recycle all that stuff?" asked Max.

"Yep," I said. "We just have to look on the package or bottle to see if it has that recycling triangle on it. If it does, then we can put it in our recycling bin."

"Good," said Mrs. Wushy. "What else?"

"We can save energy," said Robbie.

"How do you do that?" I asked.

"It's easy. You can save a lot of energy by turning off the lights when you leave a room, or turning off the TV or computer when you're done with them. Leaving your computer on wastes a lot of energy."

"My dad always forgets to turn off the lights," said Chloe.

"Well, then, you can turn them off for him," said Robbie.

"Can you think of anything else?" asked Mrs. Wushy.

"I know!" said Jessie. "We can save water."

"Saving water is very important," said Mrs. Wushy.

Jessie nodded. "My *abuela*, my grandma, always turns off the water when she brushes her teeth. She said that when she was a little girl in Mexico, her family didn't have a lot of clean water, so they had to save as much of it as they could. She also taught me to take a shower instead of a bath."

"Why?" I asked.

"You use a lot less water when you take a shower," said Jessie.

"I never knew that," I said. "I'll have to ask my mom if I can take showers from now on."

"I know something," said Chloe.

"Yes?" said Mrs. Wushy.

"We can pick up trash. I think it is really yucky when people throw their trash on the ground," said Chloe, holding her nose. "It's stinky and makes the park dirty."

"Picking up trash is a great idea," said Mrs. Wushy.

"I just thought of something else!" I said. "We can keep the air clean."

"What can kids do to keep the air clean?" asked Jessie.

"We can walk or ride our bikes instead of driving somewhere."

"We can also carpool when we go places," said Robbie, "instead of taking separate cars."

"These are all fabulous ideas," said Mrs. Wushy. "So you see that kids really can make a difference. Even the little things add up."

"But I don't do all of those things," I said.

"Me, neither," said Jessie.

"Well," said Mrs. Wushy, "over the next two days you're going to get a chance to try doing many of them during our Earth Day Challenge."

"What's that?" said Max.

"It's kind of like a contest," said Mrs. Wushy.

16

"Oooh, I love contests," said Jessie.

"Me, too," said Robbie.

"What do we have to do?" asked Max.

"It's time for recess," said Mrs. Wushy, "so I will tell you all about it when we get back to the room."

CHAPTER 2

The Challenge

When we got back to the classroom after recess, Jessie pulled a bunch of stuff out of her jacket pocket. "Look what I found on the playground, Mrs. Wushy."

"What is it, Jessie?"

"A bunch of trash: a chip bag, a candy wrapper, a napkin, and a spoon."

"Eeeewwww," said Chloe, backing away. "All that stuff is full of germs. Why did you pick it up?"

"Because it doesn't belong on the playground," said Jessie. "It belongs in a trash can. I don't know about you, but I don't want to play on a playground full of trash!"

"Good for you, Jessie," said Mrs. Wushy.

"I can't believe that all of that stuff was out there," I said. "I never noticed it before."

"Me, neither," said Jessie. "But since we started talking about taking care of our planet, I decided to look carefully today."

"It's amazing what you notice once you start looking," said Mrs. Wushy. "Maybe as part of our Earth Day activities this week, we can do a playground cleanup. What do you all think?"

"I think that sounds like a great idea!" I said. "Can we do it now?"

"Not right now," said Mrs. Wushy. "We'll do it one day later this week. Right now I want to tell you all about the Earth Day Challenge."

"I know I'm going to win," Max bragged.

"How do you know?" said Jessie.

"Because I know," said Max, sticking out his chest.

"But Mrs. Wushy hasn't even told us what it is yet," said Jessie. "Why don't you stop bragging for one minute and let Mrs. Wushy explain it?"

Max glared at Jessie.

"You might win, Max," said Mrs. Wushy.

Max grinned. "See? I told you!"

"But everyone else might win, too."

Max frowned. "What do you mean?"

"There is not going to be just one winner. If everyone works hard to take care of the planet, then everyone will be a winner."

"Even planet Earth," said Robbie, laughing.

"Even our Earth," said Mrs. Wushy.

"What do we have to do?" I asked.

Mrs. Wushy pulled out a piece of paper. "On this paper, I have listed ten things kids can do to help the planet. If you do all ten things by Friday, then you will become a member of the Green Team."

"But I don't like the color green," said Chloe. "Can I be a member of the Pink Team?"

"No," said Mrs. Wushy.

"Why not?" asked Chloe.

"Because it is called the Green Team for a reason. Has anyone ever heard someone say, 'I'm going green'?"

"Yes, but I never knew what they meant," I said.

"It means that they are doing things that are good for the planet and protecting the environment," said Robbie.

"That's right," said Mrs. Wushy. "So this week we are all going to go green!"

"Cool," said Jessie.

"Let's look at the list," said Mrs. Wushy. "Number one: Bring in some materials, such as cans and newspapers, that we can recycle by using them for projects here at school."

"That's easy," I whispered to Robbie. "We have a ton of stuff like that at my house."

"Number two: Be a power saver. Turn off all the lights when you leave a room. Also, remember to turn off the television and the computer when you are not using them."

Robbie smiled. "This is going to be easier than I thought."

"Number three: Turn off the water when you are brushing your teeth and remind other people in your family to do it, too."

"But I always leave the water running when I brush my teeth," Chloe whined. "What's so bad about that?"

"You are wasting a lot of water," said Mrs. Wushy. "If everyone turned off the water when they brushed their teeth, think about how much water we could save."

Chloe let out a big sigh.

"Number four: Bring a reusable water bottle to school instead of the plastic kind that you throw out."

"But I don't have one of those," said Max.

"Well, if you explain to your mom why it's so important to have one, then I'm sure she will buy one for you. She will end up saving a lot of money by not buying bottles of water every week."

"I never thought of that," said Jessie. "That's a good point!"

"And there will be a lot less trash," said Robbie.

"You all are catching on," said Mrs. Wushy. "Number five: Pick up ten pieces of trash in your neighborhood."

"Ten!" said Chloe. "My mom doesn't want me to touch even *one* piece of trash on the ground. It's full of germs."

"If you are worried about the germs, then you can wear a pair of gloves when you pick up the trash," said Mrs. Wushy.

"Oh, I have the perfect pair!" said Chloe. "They're pink with silvery sparkles on them!"

"Only Chloe would think about what she

was going to wear to pick up trash," Jessie whispered.

I giggled. "This doesn't seem so bad," I thought. We were halfway through the list, and the first five seemed pretty easy to do.

"Number six: Walk or ride your bike to school one day this week instead of taking the bus or riding in a car. You can find a friend or a parent to walk or ride with you."

"But I can't walk that far in my party shoes," said Chloe.

"Well, you little fancy-pants," said Max, "I guess you'll just have to wear sneakers that day."

"But sneakers don't match my party dresses. Only my party shoes do!" Chloe jumped out of her chair and twirled around so everyone could admire her outfit. "See?" she said.

"Chloe, please sit down," said Mrs. Wushy. "I need to tell the class about the last four items on the list. Number seven: Take cloth bags to the grocery store so you don't use plastic bags for your food."

"I don't have any cloth bags," said Jessie.

"Many grocery stores will give them to you for about one dollar if you ask," said Mrs. Wushy.

"I'll do that," said Jessie.

"Number eight: Use both sides of a piece of paper before you recycle it. When we save paper, we save trees," said Mrs. Wushy.

"A lot of trees are cut down every year," said Robbie.

"That's right, Robbie," said Mrs. Wushy. "Number nine: Use a cloth towel to dry your hands in the kitchen instead of a paper towel."

"You mean like a dish towel?" said Max.

"Yes," said Mrs. Wushy. "That is exactly what I mean."

"My mom already has one of those hanging in the kitchen."

"And finally, number ten: Take a shower instead of a bath."

"But I have to take a bubble bath every night," said Chloe. "My mom says that's how I keep my skin baby-soft."

"Oh brother," Jessie mumbled. "What will the princess do without her royal bath?"

"Just explain to your mother that when you take a shower, you use half as much water as when you take a bath," said Mrs. Wushy. "You can always use lotion to keep your skin soft."

Chloe frowned. "It's not the same."

"I will give you one of these challenge lists to take home. Do each of these activities sometime during the next two days and check them off as you go. If all of the activities are checked off by Friday, then you will become a member of the Green Team."

"Cool!" said Jessie. "This sounds like a lot of fun!"

"We get to have fun and help the planet at the same time," said Robbie. "Are you ready, Freddy?"

"Yeah, sure," I said, smiling weakly. I didn't know how I was going to be able to do all these things by Friday. But if I didn't do them all, then I wouldn't get to be a member of the Green Team.

I gulped. I'd have to get started as soon as I got home.

CHAPTER 3

Litterbugs

Robbie came home with me after school. We decided to pick up litter in the neighborhood together.

"How was your day, boys?" asked my mom when we walked in the door.

"Good," we both said.

"How about a snack?"

"I'd love a snack," said Robbie. "Thanks, Mrs. Thresher."

"Come on over and wash your hands in the

sink. I want to make sure they are clean before you touch any food."

We both washed our hands, and my mom started to reach for paper towels. "Wait, Mom, no!" I yelled.

"Freddy, what is the matter?" asked my mom.

"We need to dry our hands on a dish towel, not a paper towel."

"But you always dry your hands on a paper towel."

"I know, but today Mrs. Wushy was teaching us about things kids can do to help the planet. A dish towel doesn't use paper, which saves trees."

"That is good thinking," said my mom, handing us a dish towel.

I went to my backpack and pulled out the Earth Day Challenge paper. "See, Mom? We have to do all of these things by Friday. If we do, we get to be a member of the Green Team."

"These are great ideas," said my mom.

"I really want to be a member of the Green Team, but I don't know if I can do them all by Friday," I said.

"I bet you can," said my mom. "You already get to check number nine off the list."

"Oh, yeah, right," I said, smiling.

We gobbled down some cheese and crackers, drank some juice, and headed for the door.

"Where are you boys rushing off to?" asked my mom.

"We're going to pick up trash in the neighborhood," said Robbie.

"I think it's number five on the list," I said.

"Well, then you'd better each take a bag to put the trash in," said my mom. She handed us each a plastic bag from the grocery store.

"I have to remind my mom to use the cloth grocery bags," I thought. Before I could tell her, Robbie grabbed my arm. "Come on, Freddy. Let's go. We're wasting time!"

We ran out the door and started walking down the block.

"How many pieces of trash do we have to pick up?" I asked.

"I think we each have to pick up ten," said Robbie.

"Ten! That seems like a lot. I don't think our neighborhood is that dirty."

As I was talking, Robbie reached down, picked something up, and dropped it into his bag.

"What was that?"

"A gum wrapper," said Robbie. "At least it wasn't the gum. I don't see that anywhere."

"That's because it's stuck to the bottom of my shoe," I said.

"Yuck," said Robbie. "That's gross."

"Tell me about it," I said, trying to scrape the gum off with a stick.

We kept walking, and I found a candy bar

wrapper, an empty soda can, and a piece of paper.

Robbie found an old battery, a paper clip, and another soda can. "Let's go to the park and see what other trash we can find," he said.

"Good idea," I said. "Race you there!"

We took off like rockets with our bags of trash flying out behind us. I beat Robbie by a hair.

"Beat ya," I said.

"Just barely," said Robbie.

"I still beat you," I said, smiling.

We walked around the playground at the park. Robbie found a sandwich bag, a straw, and a plastic fork. "It looks like somebody finished their lunch and just dumped the trash on the ground."

"And look," I said. "The trash can is so close. It's right over there."

We both shook our heads. "People are such litterbugs," said Robbie.

I walked over to the basketball courts and found a juice box, a water bottle, and a granola bar wrapper. "I found three more pieces of trash right here," I said.

"You know, when it rains, all this trash gets washed into the storm drain," said Robbie. "Then it gets carried out to the ocean, where it pollutes the water and makes the sea animals sick."

"That's terrible," I said.

"And think about all the animals here in the park," said Robbie. "A little squirrel might think a piece of trash was something to eat, but then when he put it in his mouth, he might start choking on it."

"How sad. Poor little squirrel."

We picked up more trash in the park and then started walking back home. "Wait. We didn't check to see if we had ten pieces of trash yet," I said.

"Oh, I think we have way more than ten," said Robbie.

"I never realized how many litterbugs we had in our neighborhood," I said.

"Me, neither," said Robbie.

We walked past Mrs. Golden's house. Her dog, Baxter, leaped off the front porch to greet us.

"Hey, Baxter. Hey, buddy. How are you?" I said, petting his head.

Baxter wagged his tail and stuck his nose in my bag.

"No, buddy. That's not for you," I said, pulling the bag away.

"What's in the bag?" asked Mrs. Golden.

"Trash," we both said.

"Why do you boys have bags of trash?"

"We are trying to clean up the neighborhood and protect the planet," Robbie said.

"We are doing an Earth Day challenge for school," I said. "We want to be members of the Green Team."

"Good for you, boys," said Mrs. Golden. "It's important to take care of this beautiful planet that we live on."

Baxter ran to the neighbor's lawn, picked up a piece of paper in his mouth, trotted back over to where we were standing, and dropped the paper at my feet.

"I think Baxter also wants to be a member of the Green Team," said Mrs. Golden.

We all laughed.

"Good boy, Baxter," I said, rubbing his back. "Thanks for the paper." I picked it up and put it in my bag.

"Well, we'd better be going, Mrs. Golden," Robbie said.

"Keep up the good work, boys," she said.

When we arrived at my house, it was time for Robbie to go home. "Well, now we can check number five off our list," he said.

"That's two down. Eight more to go," I said with a big sigh.

"See you tomorrow, Freddy, for our walk to school."

"Yep, see you tomorrow."

CHAPTER 4

Walk, Don't Drive

The next morning I heard my mom yelling at me from downstairs. "Freddy, you need to get a move on. Remember, you're walking to school today."

Oh no! I had almost forgotten! I jumped out of bed, threw on my clothes, and ran into the bathroom. I accidentally bumped into my sister, Suzie, who was brushing her teeth. Her toothbrush flew out of her hand and landed in the toilet.

"Now look what you did, you little pain," said Suzie. "Why don't you watch where you're going?"

"Sorry," I said. "I'll get it for you." I reached into the toilet and pulled out her toothbrush. "Here you go."

"Are you kidding me? I'm not going to use

that toothbrush ever again! That's disgusting! And I can't believe you stuck your hand in the toilet. Wait until I tell Mom."

"You wouldn't do that," I said.

"Oh really? Watch me. She'll flip out. You know what a neat freak she is."

"Please don't tell her."

"What's it worth to you?"

"How about I let you control the remote for the television for two nights?"

"Two nights? Make it a week, and we have a deal," she said, holding up her pinkie for a pinkie swear.

"A week? That's not fair!"

"Then I'll tell Mom as soon as we get downstairs."

"Fine," I said, "a week." I reached for Suzie's pinkie, but she pulled it back. "Now what?"

"No pinkie swear until you wash that hand you stuck in the toilet!"

I washed my hands and then we locked pinkies.

"Now go get me another toothbrush," Suzie demanded.

I tossed her toothbrush in the trash can and got out a new one. "Here you go," I said, handing her the clean toothbrush.

She started brushing her teeth again.

"You shouldn't leave the water running when you brush your teeth," I said.

"What?" said Suzie.

"You shouldn't leave the faucet running. It wastes a lot of water. You should turn it off while you're brushing."

"What are you? The water police?"

"No, I'm learning about things kids can do to help the planet. Mrs. Wushy gave us an Earth Day Challenge list, and that was number three. If I do all of the things on the list by Friday, then I get to be a member of the Green Team."

"That sounds kind of cool," said Suzie as she turned off the water.

"It is. That's also why I am walking to school today. That's number six on the list. Walking means fewer cars and less pollution in the air."

"Freddy," called my mom. "If you don't come down right this instant, then you're going to have to take the bus."

I couldn't take the bus. If I did, then I

wouldn't be able to cross number six off the list. "Coming, Mom!" I yelled.

Suzie followed me out of the bathroom. I stopped, turned to her, and said, "Uh, I think you forgot something."

"Now what, Mr. Green Jeans?"

"You forgot to turn off the light. You should always turn off the light when you leave a room. You want to be a power saver, not a power waster."

Suzie went back into the bathroom and turned off the light.

"Thanks for taking care of the planet," I said, smiling. That was one more thing I could check off the challenge list.

I bounded down the stairs and into the kitchen.

"What took you so long, and what were you and Suzie arguing about?" my mom asked.

"Nothing," I said. "I was just reminding her to turn the faucet off when she brushes her teeth. You know, you and Dad should do that, too. You can save a lot of water that way."

"I'll try to remember to do that tonight," said my dad, looking up from his paper.

I looked up at the clock. "Robbie is going to be here any minute! I'd better take my bagel to go, Mom. I'll just eat it while I'm walking."

The doorbell rang. "There's Robbie now." I grabbed my bagel and my shark backpack and ran to the front door.

"Ready, Freddy?" asked Robbie.

"Yep," I said with my mouth full of bagel. A few pieces of food flew out of my mouth. "Eewww, gross," said Robbie. "Say it, don't spray it," he said, laughing.

I smiled and nodded.

We started to walk down the street.

"I think I actually like walking better than riding the bus," Robbie said.

"Yeah," I said. "We don't have to listen to Max or Chloe."

Just then we heard a familiar voice.

"Heh, heh, watch out, suckers!" yelled Max as he sped by on his bicycle.

"He's the one who should watch out," said Robbie.

"Yeah," I said. "He almost ran us over."

"See you losers at school," Max called over his shoulder.

Just then Jessie stepped out in front of Max's bike, and he had to slam on the brakes.

She took hold of his handlebars and said, "Hey, loser. Why don't you slow down and watch where *you're* going? You almost ran over my friends."

"Let go of my bike," said Max.

"I'll let go as soon as you say you're sorry."

"Sorry," Max mumbled.

"What was that? I couldn't hear you."

"Sorry!" Max yelled.

"That's better," said Jessie. She let go of his handlebars. "Run along now," she said.

Max took off like a speeding bullet.

Jessie was so brave. She was the only one who would stand up to Max, the biggest bully in the whole first grade.

"Thanks, Jessie," I said.

"No problem. He thinks he's so tough," said Jessie. "But he's really just a big baby."

We all laughed.

"We'd better start running if we're going

to make it to school in time for the first bell," said Robbie.

"Let's race," said Jessie. "On your mark. Get set. Go!"

I ran as fast as I could. I thought my heart was going to pop out of my chest, but Jessie still beat us both.

"You are amazing!" I said to Jessie, giving her a high five.

"Thanks," she said, and smiled.

CHAPTER 5

Plant a Tree

When we got to our classroom, Mrs. Wushy asked, "How many of you walked or rode your bikes to school today?"

A bunch of hands shot up, and there was a chorus of "I did! I did! I did!"

"Wow! That's great!" said Mrs. Wushy. "Good for you."

"I thought it was really fun," said Jessie.

"Me, too," I said.

"Robbie, Freddy, and I had a race to school," said Jessie.

"Ha-ha. That's funny," said Max. "I bet they beat the pants off of you!"

"Actually, Jessie beat us both," said Robbie.

"No way. A girl can't run faster than a boy," said Max.

"Says who?" said Jessie.

"Says me," said Max.

"Well, you're wrong," said Jessie. "Girls can run just as fast as boys."

"That's right," said Mrs. Wushy. "Girls can be very fast runners."

"Jessie is probably the fastest kid in the whole first grade," I said.

Jessie smiled.

"Where's Chloe?" asked Mrs. Wushy.

"I'm over here!" Chloe called from the cubbies.

"What are you doing?" Mrs. Wushy asked.

"Changing my shoes."

"Did she say, 'Changing my shoes'?" Robbie whispered.

I nodded. "Yep. You heard her right."

"I had to wear my sneakers to walk to school today, but they don't match my outfit," said Chloe. "I'm taking them off and putting on these pink party shoes instead. Aren't they beautiful? And they match perfectly with my dress."

"She is so weird," Jessie whispered.

"Well, you might want to leave your sneakers on, Chloe, because right now we're going to go outside and plant a few trees," said Mrs. Wushy.

"Really?" I said excitedly.

"Really," said Mrs. Wushy.

"That is so cool," said Max.

"But my dress is going to get all dirty," said Chloe.

"Then maybe you shouldn't wear your foofy dresses to school," said Max.

"But my nana just brought this one back from Paris, France."

"I'm sure if you get a little dirt on it, your mother can wash it," said Mrs. Wushy.

Chloe frowned. "I don't like dirt."

"I love it," said Max. "And I love all of the things that live in the dirt, like worms and bugs."

"Ewww, ewww, ewww!" said Chloe.

"Enough, you two," said Mrs. Wushy. "Let's all line up to go outside and plant some trees."

We got in a line and followed Mrs. Wushy out to the playground.

"One of our local stores donated these baby trees to our school. I thought we could use more shade on our playground," said Mrs. Wushy.

"Good idea!" I said. "It can get really hot out here."

"When these baby trees get a little bigger, we can sit under them and cool off," said Jessie.

"Besides giving us shade, does anyone know other reasons why trees are important?" asked Mrs. Wushy.

"They make oxygen that we need to

breathe," said Robbie. "If we didn't have oxygen to breathe, then we would die."

"Really?" said Max.

"Really," said Mrs. Wushy.

"Wow! I never knew that," said Max.

"These trees will also help us in another way," said Mrs. Wushy. "You know how the field gets very muddy when there's a lot of rain?"

We nodded.

"That's because all of the soil around the grass gets washed onto the field. If we plant the trees around the field, then the roots of the trees will help hold the soil in place, and it won't all wash onto the grass. You won't have to run around in muddy pools of water."

"I always thought that trees were pretty to look at," said Jessie. "I didn't realize how important they were."

"And nine hundred million trees are cut down every year," said Mrs. Wushy.

"Why?" I asked.

"To make paper products."

I shook my head. "That's crazy."

Jessie shook her head, too. "I just can't believe that."

"If you use less paper, then fewer trees have to be cut down," said Mrs. Wushy. "It's that simple. Now, is everybody ready to get started?"

"Yes!" we all said. Well, everybody except Chloe.

Mrs. Wushy put us in groups of five and gave each group a big shovel and one of the baby trees.

"You need to dig a deep enough hole so that we can set the tree down in the ground. Then, once the tree is in the ground, you cover the roots up with dirt. Got it?" she said.

"Got it!" we all said.

We spread out around the track and got to work. Digging the hole was hard, but really fun.

"Hey, look what I found!" said Robbie, sticking his hand in the dirt and pulling out a bug. "A roly-poly."

"It's so cute," said Jessie. "Can I hold it?"

"Sure," said Robbie.

"Cute? How can you say that disgusting thing is cute?" said Chloe. "I wouldn't touch it if you paid me a million dollars!"

"You don't know what you're missing," said Jessie with a big smile on her face.

"Hey, Chloe," said Max. "Come over here. I've got a surprise for you."

Chloe ran over. "I just love surprises!"

Max pulled a big, fat worm out of his pocket and dangled it in Chloe's face.

Chloe screamed, "AAAAAAHHHHHH!" and ran over to Mrs. Wushy. "Mrs. Wushy! Mrs. Wushy! Max just stuck a worm in my face."

"I think you'll be all right," said Mrs. Wushy. "It's just a little worm. Worms are important for the environment, you know."

"Well, I don't like them," said Chloe. "They are slimy and gross."

"Okay, everybody, it's time to go inside. Bring your shovels over to me and line up," called Mrs Wushy.

"Boy oh boy, the morning went quickly," said Robbie.

"Time flies when you are having fun," said Mrs. Wushy. "It's already time for lunch."

"Woohoo!" I yelled, and pumped my fist in the air. "I'm starving."

"I'm going to ask you a special favor while you're at lunch today," said Mrs. Wushy. "Please save all of your trash and bring it back to the classroom with you. I want to talk about it."

CHAPTER 6

Worms and Trash

When the bell rang for the end of lunch, Chloe was about to throw out all her trash. "Wait!" said Jessie, pulling her back from the trash can. "Remember, Mrs. Wushy said we're supposed to bring all of our trash back to the classroom."

"But it's sticky and gross, and it's going to make my lunch box all stinky," said Chloe, wrinkling up her nose.

"You are such a princess," said Jessie, shaking her head. "Just give me your trash. I'll carry it for you."

When we got back to the classroom, Mrs. Wushy had put some newspaper down on the floor. "Please put your lunch trash on these papers," she said.

We all pulled out our trash and piled it up on the floor.

"Wow! That's a lot of trash," said Jessie.

"You can say that again," I said.

"Think about what you throw away every day at lunch," said Mrs. Wushy.

"My sandwich bag," said Jessie.

"The wrapper from my granola bar," I said.

"My napkin," said Max.

"I didn't even know he used a napkin," I whispered to Jessie.

Jessie giggled.

"The bag from my chips," said Robbie.

"Now think about how much trash every

school collects in one day," said Mrs. Wushy. "All of that goes into landfills."

"What's a landfill?" said Chloe.

"It's a big hole in the ground where we throw all the trash that the garbage people collect," Mrs. Wushy said.

"There are a lot of landfills," said Robbie.

"Yes, there are," said Mrs. Wushy. "If we aren't careful, soon our planet will be covered in trash. And this trash pollutes the air and water."

"That's disgusting," said Chloe.

"But what can we do?" said Jessie.

"All of this trash does not have to go into the landfill," said Mrs. Wushy.

"What do you mean?" said Max.

"Well, some of this stuff can be recycled," said Robbie.

"Now you're on the right track," said Mrs. Wushy. "If you have anything that can be recycled, then put it over here on this paper."

"I have a water bottle," Max said.

I leaned over to Robbie and whispered, "I brought a reusable water bottle today." That was number four on the challenge list.

"Me, too," Robbie whispered back.

"I have the plastic container from my applesauce," said Jessie.

Max poked Chloe. "Hey, Ding-Dong, you have something that goes in the recycling pile."

"Keep your dirty little hands off of me," said Chloe. "None of my trash can be recycled."

"Yes, it can," said Max.

"Oh yeah? What?" said Chloe, glaring at Max.

"Uh, your yogurt container."

"No, it can't."

"Yes, it can."

"No, it can't."

"Yes, it can," said Max.

"Enough, you two," said Mrs. Wushy. "Yes, Chloe, your yogurt container can be recycled."

"Well, my mom never recycles them at home."

"Now that you know it can be recycled," said Mrs. Wushy, "you can tell your mom."

Jessie picked up the container and put it in the recycling pile.

"Thank you, Jessie," said Mrs. Wushy.

Jessie smiled. "No problem. This is fun!"

"Now, is there anything else we can do with this trash?" asked Mrs. Wushy.

We all stared at Mrs. Wushy and shook our

heads. Well, all of us except Robbie, the science genius.

"We could compost some of this stuff," said Robbie.

"Hey, Brain," said Max, "what's compost?"

"You'd like it," said Robbie, "because composting uses worms."

"Cool!" said Max.

"EEEEEEWWWWW!" said Chloe. "I hate worms."

"But they help make the soil really good for planting," said Robbie.

"That's right," said Mrs. Wushy. "If you have a compost bin, then you can throw some of your food trash in there, like this leftover sandwich crust or this banana peel."

"But isn't that just like throwing it away?" I said.

"Not exactly," said Mrs. Wushy. "If you throw the food scraps in the compost, then the worms break down the food and use it to make really rich soil that is good for your garden."

"Cool!" said Max. "I wish I could see one."

"If you want to make a small compost bin for our classroom, I can show you how to do that tomorrow," said Mrs. Wushy.

"Yes! Yes! Yes!" we all said.

"They are really very easy to make. I will bring in the bin. The bottom has to be lined with newspaper, so if you could all bring in some newspaper to make the worm bedding, that would be great."

"I have lots of newspaper in my recycle bin at home," I said.

"Me, too!" said Robbie.

"Besides," said Mrs. Wushy, "recycling is number one on the Earth Day Challenge list. If you bring in newspaper, then you are one step closer to becoming a member of the Green Team. Remember, the challenge ends tomorrow."

The challenge! I was having so much fun today I almost forgot about the challenge. Time was running out, and I still had four more things to do!

CHAPTER 7

Reduce, Reuse, Recycle

When I got home from school, my mom said, "I have to run to the grocery store. Do you want to go with me, Freddy?"

"Sure, Mom," I said.

"I'm just going to jot down a quick grocery list." My mom reached for a new piece of paper.

"Wait, Mom," I said. "Use this." I handed her a paper that had a note written on one side.

"But this paper has something on it already."

"But only on one side. You can write your list on the other side," I said.

"You're right, Freddy. Why waste a perfectly clean piece of paper for my list? I can certainly use this piece you gave me."

I smiled. Using two sides of a paper was number eight on the list.

"All right. I think I'm ready," said my mom as she finished writing. "Let's go. I have to buy some things for dinner and start cooking, or we're never going to eat tonight." She started toward the door.

"Mom, you forgot something again."

"What did I forget this time?"

"The cloth grocery bags," I said.

"Good thing you reminded me," she said. "I almost never remember them until I'm at the grocery store, and by then, it's too late."

"You should just leave them in the trunk all the time. Then you'll always have them with you," I said.

"How did you get to be so smart?" Mom said, giving me a hug.

Bringing cloth bags to the grocery store was number seven on the list. I was almost done. Only two more to go!

Later that night, after a delicious dinner of spaghetti and meatballs, I announced, "It's time to get clean!"

"Freddy, honey, are you feeling all right?" asked my mom.

"What do you mean?" I said.

"I don't think I've ever heard you say you *wanted* to take a bath."

"Not a bath. A shower," I said.

"A shower?" asked Suzie. "Since when is Freddy allowed to take a shower?"

"It's none of your beeswax," I said.

"Yes, it is," said Suzie.

"No, it's not."

"Yes, it is."

"No, it's not."

"Stop it, both of you," said my dad. "Freddy, since when do you take showers?"

"Since I found out that taking a shower uses up half as much water as taking a bath," I said.

"I never knew that," said my dad. "Where did you learn that?"

"In school. So can I take a shower?"

"Sure," said my dad.

"That's not fair!" said Suzie. "What about me?"

"You can, too," said my dad. "We all have to do our part to help the planet."

I turned to Suzie. "You're welcome," I said.

My mom followed me upstairs and helped me take my very first shower. I loved feeling the water sprinkling down on my head. It felt like I was standing out in the rain without an umbrella.

"That was awesome!" I said as I stepped out of the shower. "I want to do that every night!"

My mom laughed. "Glad you enjoyed it. Now get your pajamas on before you catch a cold. I'm going back downstairs to wash the dinner dishes."

I put on my pajamas and went to my room

to get the Earth Day Challenge list so my mom and dad could sign it. I was proud of myself for doing everything on the list. I glanced down at the paper, and my heart skipped a beat. I had forgotten to do number one on the list: Bring recyclable items to school.

"No problem," I thought. "That's an easy one." I was supposed to bring newspaper for the compost tomorrow, anyway. I just had to go get some from the recycling bin in the garage.

I ran downstairs into the garage and started digging through the recycling bin for newspapers.

"Freddy, Freddy, is that you?" my mom called from the kitchen.

"Yeah, Mom, it's me!" I called back.

"What's all that noise?"

"I'm looking for something," I said as I continued throwing cans and empty containers onto the ground behind me.

I couldn't find any newspaper. Now I was starting to panic. What if we didn't have any? If I didn't bring in any newspapers tomorrow, then I wouldn't get to be a member of the Green Team.

My mom walked into the garage. "What are you doing out here? I can barely see you." She turned on the light. "Freddy, look at this mess you're making! What are you doing? And why are you out here in the dirty garage after you have already taken a shower?"

"I—I—I—" I stammered.

"You need to tell me right now," my mom demanded.

"I'm sorry, Mom," I said as a tear rolled down my cheek. "I just wanted . . . Earth Day Challenge . . . Green Team," I sniffled.

"Freddy, calm down," my mom said. "I don't understand a word you're saying. Take a deep breath and then try again."

I took a deep breath and wiped my nose on my pajama sleeve. "If I don't bring newspaper to school tomorrow, then I won't have done all ten things on the Earth Day Challenge list, so I won't get to be a member of the Green Team."

"Well, why didn't you just say so?" said my mom.

"We always have newspaper out here in this bin, but I just can't find any."

"That's because I pulled all of it out for a Girl Scout project your sister's troop is going to do next week," my mom said.

"Can I have some?" I asked.

"Of course you can, honey. Before we go back in the house, I'll help you put all of this stuff you threw on the floor back into the recycling bin."

"Thanks, Mom," I said as we threw everything back in.

"What do you need the newspaper for, anyway?" asked my mom.

"We're going to be making a compost bin in our classroom tomorrow. The newspaper is the bedding for the worms."

"That sounds really interesting. I can't wait

to hear all about it when you get home from school tomorrow."

We went back inside, and my mom gave me some newspaper. "Here you go, Freddy. Is that everything on your list?"

"Yep," I said, grinning. "You just have to sign it, and then when I give it to Mrs. Wushy tomorrow, I'll be a member of the Green Team!"

CHAPTER 8

Go Green!

The next day we were all putting our back-packs away in our cubbies when Chloe started running around the room, screaming, "AAAAAAHHHHHHHH!"

"Chloe," said Mrs. Wushy, "what's wrong?"

"There's a . . . there's a . . . there's a worm in my cubby."

Max started laughing hysterically: "HA, HA, HA, HA, HA!"

"Chloe, calm down," said Mrs. Wushy. "It's not going to do anything to you."

Chloe covered her eyes. "I can't look at it. Just get it out! Get it out!" she screamed.

Mrs. Wushy slowly pulled the worm out of Chloe's cubby and held it in her hand. "It's out now, Chloe. You can open your eyes."

"Throw it outside! Throw it outside!" said Chloe.

"Actually, this worm is going to go in the compost bin we make today. It's called a red wiggler. I got some last night. This little guy must have escaped from the jar I was keeping them in."

"Can we make the compost bin right now?" asked Jessie.

"Sure," said Mrs. Wushy. "If you brought newspapers in today, please bring them over to the rug."

We all got out the newspaper we had brought.

Mrs. Wushy carried a big plastic bin to the rug. "This is going to be our compost bin. I poked some holes in the lid. Does anybody know why?"

"So that the worms have air to breathe," said Robbie.

"That's right," said Mrs. Wushy. "Now we have to line the bottom with damp paper shreds."

"What do we do with the newspaper?" I asked.

"That's going to be the worm bedding," said

Mrs. Wushy. "You all need to rip the paper into one-inch-wide strips."

We all started ripping. "This is fun!" said Jessie.

"Now we make it a little bit damp by spraying some water on it, and then spread it out on the bottom of the bin."

"What next?" asked Max.

"We add some dead leaves, some grass clippings, and some food scraps, like this banana peel, this orange rind, and these crushed eggshells."

"But that's garbage!" said Chloe. "Why are we putting stinky garbage in the bin?"

"Because that's what the worms like to eat," said Mrs. Wushy.

Chloe held her nose. "P.U.," she said.

"Finally," said Mrs. Wushy, "we add the worms. They like to be buried under the paper and food scraps, so we'll stick them under there."

"Now what?" I said.

"Now the worms break down the rotting plants and food into a dark, rich soil that's good for planting."

"That's amazing," said Jessie.

"Now I think it's time to see who finished the Earth Day Challenge," said Mrs. Wushy. "If you completed the list, then please go get it and bring it to back to the rug."

The whole class jumped up to get their papers.

"Now let's see," said Mrs. Wushy. "Who finished the challenge?"

Everyone's hand shot up.

"I did! I did!" everyone shouted out.

"Really?" asked Mrs. Wushy. *"Everyone* completed everything on the list? Congratulations! That's fantastic! You are all amazing."

"What do I win?" asked Chloe. "A pony?"

"A pony?" said Max. "You're crazy!"

"I am not crazy. Besides, I wasn't talking to you," said Chloe. "I was talking to Mrs. Wushy."

"No, Chloe," said Mrs. Wushy. "In this challenge, *you* don't win anything. The Earth does."

"What do you mean?"

"The Earth will be a better place because of you," said Mrs. Wushy.

"Oh," said Chloe, pouting. "I thought I won a prize."

"Well, everybody does get a pin that says 'The Green Team.'"

Mrs. Wushy handed out the pins.

"Cool!" I said.

"Can we put them on now?" asked Jessie.

"Of course you can," said Mrs. Wushy. "You should wear it proudly."

I pinned mine to my shirt and smiled.

"Remember," said Mrs. Wushy, "we should take care of the Earth every day, not just on Earth Day. Now you all know lots of ways to protect our planet, and you can share them with your friends and family."

"They are all so simple," said Jessie.

"Yeah," I said. "I thought the challenge was going to be really hard, but it was actually pretty easy."

"Like I said before," said Mrs. Wushy, "even little things add up to make the world a better place."

DEAR READER,

We are lucky to live on such a beautiful planet, and we need to do everything we can to protect it. Did you know that there are many things kids just like you can do to make the world a better place?

If you love the Earth, and all the things that live on it, then find a way to help. A great place to start is Scholastic's Act Green website: **Scholastic.com/actgreen**. This website lists over one hundred things kids can do to be more green and help the environment. Just like Freddy, you and your class can become members of the Green Team.

So get involved and make your voice heard! Participate in a neighborhood cleanup, make a compost bin for your home or classroom, or start a Green Team club at your school. One person can make a difference.

Hope you have as much fun reading *Save the Earth!* as I had writing it.

HAPPY READING!

Freddy's Fun Pages

FREDDY'S SHARK JOURNAL

SHARKS NEED PROTECTING

Not everyone loves sharks as much as Freddy does. Did you know that even this mighty creature of the sea needs our help to survive?

Every year as many as one hundred million sharks are killed.

Humans kill sharks for sport and food, and sometimes by mistake.

Soup made from shark fins is popular in some parts of the world. Hunters cut off the shark's fin and then throw the shark back into the water to die.

Fishermen drop huge nets into the water to catch fish like tuna, but sharks get caught in the nets and die.

Some hunters kill sharks so they can sell their large jaws as souvenirs.

We need to protect sharks and their environment!

JOIN THE GREEN TEAM!

Can you complete the Earth Day Challenge?

1. Recycle cans, plastic, paper, and glass.

2. Be a power saver: Turn off lights, computers, and the television when you leave the room.

3. Turn off the water when brushing your teeth.

4. Use a reusable water bottle.

5. Pick up litter on your playground or in your neighborhood.

6. Walk or ride your bike to school as much as possible.

7. Use cloth bags instead of plastic at the grocery store.

8. Use two sides of a piece of paper before recycling it.

9. Use a cloth dish towel to dry your hands instead of a paper towel.

10. Take a shower instead of a bath.

Go, Green Team!

WIGGLY, WIGGLY WORMS

Make a compost bin for your house
or classroom. It's easy!

YOU WILL NEED:

White glue
A large plastic bin
Newspaper and cardboard
Dead leaves, grass, weeds, food scraps (banana
     peels, eggshells, potato peelings, etc.)
Red wigglers (This is the only kind of worm
     you should use in a compost bin. You can
     find them at a bait shop or ask your parents
     to order some online.)

DIRECTIONS:

1. Poke holes in the top of the bin so the
worms can breathe.

2. Rip pieces of newspaper and cardboard
into one-inch-wide strips and lay them on
the bottom of the bin to make the worm
bedding. Spray the bedding with water to
make it damp.

3. Add the dead leaves, grass, and food scraps, and bury them with the bedding.

4. Add the red wigglers.

5. Put on the lid so the worms won't escape, and add more leaves and scraps daily to keep the worms fed.

6. The worms will turn the rotting leaves and food into compost. Mix the compost into the soil when you are planting to help plants grow healthy and strong!

DON'T BE A LITTERBUG!

Make these cute litterbugs out of recycled materials to remind your friends NOT to be litterbugs.

YOU WILL NEED:

An egg carton

Glue, tape, and scissors

Materials to recycle, such as straws, foam
   packing pieces, bottle caps, paper clips,
   string, and anything else you can think of
Markers

DIRECTIONS:

1. Cut two egg cups off the egg carton. Turn them open side down and tape or glue them together. They will be the head and body of your litterbug.

2. Make two antennae from paper clips or packing foam pieces.

3. Cut straws to desired length to make six legs, and poke holes in the egg cups to stick them into the body (three on each side).

4. Glue two bottle caps onto the head for eyes.

5. Glue a piece of string onto the head for the mouth, or draw a mouth with a marker.

6. Decorate your litterbug by drawing crazy designs on it with your markers.

7. Tape a sign to its back that says "Don't be a litterbug!"

Have you read all about Freddy?

Don't miss any of Freddy's funny adventures!